Big Boy,
Little Boy

Big Boy,
Little Boy

by Betty Jo Stanovich
illustrated by Virginia Wright-Frierson

Lothrop, Lee & Shepard Books
New York

Text copyright © 1984 by Betty Jo Stanovich
Illustrations copyright © 1984 by Virginia Wright-Frierson

Library of Congress Cataloging in Publication Data
Stanovich, Betty Jo.   Big boy, little boy.   Summary: A four-year-old
who is newly independent gets Grandma to help him remember when
he was a "little boy."   [1. Growth—Fiction.   2. Grandmothers—
Fiction]   I. Wright-Frierson, Virginia, ill.   II. Title.
PZ7.S7932Bi   1984   [E]   83-26773
ISBN 0-688-03807-7   ISBN 0-688-03808-5 (lib. bdg.)

For David, Katie, Brian, Kian, Quita, Michael, Christopher,
and all big-little children everywhere.
With special thanks and love to all my good friends—B.J.S.

For Dargan Michael and my parents. With love to
D.F. and my families and thanks to Ann.—V.W.-F.

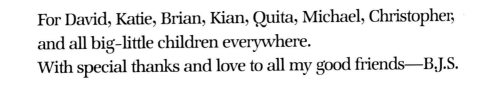

David dumped all the blocks onto the rug.
"Grandma," he said, "come build with me."

"Not now," said Grandma. "I am busy, but I will watch you build."

So David built a great big train.
He made it go clickety-clack
down the railroad tracks.

Then David got out Grandpa's tools.
"Grandma," he said,
"come hammer with me."

"Not now," said Grandma. "I am busy, but I will watch you hammer."

So David raised the big hammer and banged the post into its hole.
Grandma nodded and watched.

Then David followed Grandma outside.

"Grandma," he said, "come draw with me."

"Not now," said Grandma. "I am still busy,
but you can draw something for me."

So, back inside, David drew a pond and some flowers and some ducks. Then he drew himself and his grandma by the pond.

"That is lovely," said Grandma, sitting down beside him. "Just lovely."

"Grandma," David said, "talk to me."

"Well, David," said Grandma, "I've been thinking."

"What about, Grandma?" David asked.

"I've been thinking about how you are such a big boy now," replied Grandma.

David smiled.

"You can build trains," said Grandma.
"Great big trains that go clickety-clack.

You can hammer better than I can hammer. And you can draw such fine pictures."

"I can even stand on
my head," David said.
And he did.

"And I was remembering," Grandma went on,
"back to when you were a little boy. Do you remember?"

"I'm not sure," David said,
  liking this part best.

"You were not nearly so tall as you are now," said Grandma.
"And you couldn't even write your name."

"I couldn't?" David said, making his eyes wide.

"And I used to make up stories
for you," said Grandma,
the corners of her mouth
tugging upward.

"You did?" said David,
climbing into Grandma's lap.

Grandma nodded, then added,
"And I used to hold you
in my arms and sing you
to sleep."

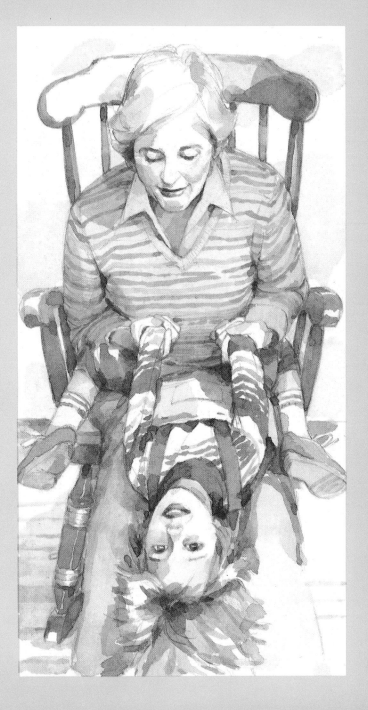

David was quiet for a while.
"Grandma," he finally said, "I am thinking
that maybe I don't remember being little at all."

"Well, then," said Grandma, "shall I tell you a story?"

"Yes, yes," David agreed. "That is sure to help me remember."

So David nestled his head into Grandma's shoulder
while she told him a favorite story
about when she was a little girl
and sat near the window in the summer sun.

"Almost," said David, yawning. "I almost remember."

"Well, then," said Grandma, "shall I sing to you?"

"Yes, yes," said David. "That might help me remember best of all."

So Grandma sang and rocked, sang and rocked.

And, in his dreams, David remembered.